Stories from Scotland

Book 1 by Moira Miller

Oliver & Boyd

Language consultant for the series, Glenys M. Smith

Acknowledgments
We are grateful to the following for supplying photographs and information and giving permission for their use: BBC Hulton Picture Library, p. 26; Janet & Colin Bord, p. 33 (three); Forestry Commission, p. 127 (two); Jarrold Colour Publications, p. 128 (foot); Hamish MacInnes, p. 72; National Trust for Scotland, cover; Photo Library International – Leeds, pp. 49, 84; Scottish Tourist Board, pp. 20, 32, 42, 61, 120, 121, 128 (top two); The Scotsman Publications Ltd., p. 82; Topham, p. 41.

Illustrated by Leonora Box, Nancy Bryce, Peter Cornwell, Graham Forbes, John Harrold, Nicholas Hewetson, Harry Horse, Annabel Large, Jim Russell, Michael Strand, Patricia Tourret.

Oliver & Boyd
Robert Stevenson House
1–3 Baxter's Place
Leith Walk
Edinburgh EH1 3BB

A Division of Longman Group Ltd

ISBN 0 05 003562 2

First published 1985

© Moira Miller 1985

Set in 14/20pt Monophoto Plantin
Produced by Longman Group (FE) Ltd
Printed in Hong Kong

Contents

Whuppity Stoorie

Once upon a time, there was
a poor woman. She lived with her
baby son in a little cottage
at Kittlerumpit. In a small garden
round the cottage she grew potatoes
and turnips. They had nothing else
to eat, but in a pigsty
at the back of the cottage
she kept a fat old pig.
She hoped to sell him
at the market.

One morning, when she went out
to feed the pig,
she found him lying on his side.
She pushed and poked,
but he was too old and ill to get up.

"Owwwwwwww!" cried the poor woman.
"I was going to sell the pig
and buy food and clothes
for the winter. Who will buy a pig
too old and ill to stand up?"
She sat down and pulled her apron
over her head, crying and howling.

She made so much noise
that she didn't see an old woman
come towards her out of the trees.
The woman was tall and thin.
She wore a long green dress
and a black cloak.
On her head was a black hat,
which made her look even taller.
She marched up to the poor woman
and poked her.

"Hoots, woman!" she shouted.
"What is all this fuss?
I could hear you over the other side
of the hill. What's the meaning of it?"

The poor woman stopped crying and stared.

"Who are you?" she sniffed.
"I've never seen you here before."

"Nosey-poke, some folk!"
snapped the tall old woman.
"Ask no questions, I'll tell no lies.
Now what is all this about?"

The poor woman told her
about the pig.

"I was going to sell him
to buy food and clothes for the winter.
But who will buy a pig
too old and ill to stand up?"
She started to cry all over again.

"We'll see about that," said
the tall fairy. For that is
what she was. She went into the
pigsty and took a small bottle
from her bag. She rubbed the pig's

6

nose and the tip of his tail
with oil from the bottle.
At the same time
she whispered some words
which the poor woman couldn't hear.
Then she poked the pig with her stick.

"Get up, you silly old grumphie!"
the fairy ordered. "And stop your nonsense,
this minute!"

The pig rolled on to his feet.
He started to eat his food
just as if nothing had been wrong.

The poor woman was delighted.
"Oh thank you, thank you!"
she said,
clapping her hands.
"What can I do for you?
I have no money,
but you could have some

potatoes or turnips from the garden.
If your Fairyship will just wait
I'll make a cup of tea."

But the fairy held up her hand.

"Stop it, woman," she ordered.
"I have no need of potatoes or
turnips, or even a cup of tea.
I need only one thing."

"Name it," said the poor woman,
"and it's yours."

"I want your son," said the fairy.

"Oh no!" howled the poor woman.
"Not my baby, my poor wee baby.
Please – take anything you like,
but not my baby."

But the fairy wouldn't listen
to her.

"You have three days
to guess my name," she said.
"If you guess wrong,
the baby is mine. Three days, mind you."
She stamped her foot,
waved her stick, and vanished.

For the whole of the first day
the poor woman sat in the cottage
hugging her baby and crying.
On the second day
she had to go out
to gather more wood for the fire.
She climbed the hill behind the house,
up into the trees.
On and on she walked.

At last she found herself in
a part of the forest
where she had never been before.
It was dark among the trees
and very quiet.

Here the birds did not sing
as they did round the cottage.
But there was another sound.

The poor woman stood still
and listened. She could hear
the hum of a spinning-wheel,
and a voice singing.

As she crept through the trees
towards the sound,
she suddenly saw a cave.
Sitting at the mouth of the cave,
with her spinning wheel, was –
the wicked fairy!

She was spinning and singing to herself.

These were the words that she was
singing, over and over again.

"Little knows that silly old dame,
That Whuppity Stoorie is my name."

The poor woman laughed to herself.
She crept back through the trees
and ran down the hill
as fast as she could go.

Next morning, when the fairy came for
the baby, she found the poor woman
sitting by the cottage door.
She was howling and crying
louder than ever.

"Hoots!" shouted the fairy. "What a noise!"
But it will do no good.
"I *will* have that baby."

The poor woman howled even louder.

"Take my pig," she cried.
"Take all the potatoes and turnips.
Take me! But leave my baby.
Please leave him!"

"Take you!" screeched the fairy.

"What would I want with you?
There would never be
a minute's peace again
with all your howling.
I have come for the baby
and I will have him."

Then the poor woman jumped up
and laughed.

"Just a minute!" she shouted.
"You think I'm not good enough.
You think I'm not fit
to tie the shoe laces of the
      Great-Lady-Snooty –

WHUPPITY STOORIE!!

As soon as the fairy heard her name
she screeched so loud that
all the birds flew from the forest
in fright. She jumped on her stick
and vanished in a great wind that
tossed the trees as if they were grass.

The poor woman laughed
and hugged her baby.

"I don't think we'll see her
any more," she said.
And she was quite right.
Whuppity Stoorie was never seen again,
either in Kittlerumpit or anywhere else.

Alan's Garden

Alan's big sister Janet was very clever.

She did the shopping for Mum.

She counted the money herself.

She never forgot which things to buy.

"You *are* clever," said Mum and Dad.

"I want to do the shopping," said Alan.

"All right," said Mum.

She gave him the money
and asked him to buy some bread.

On the way he stopped to watch
the dustbin men with the new
yellow lorry. He forgot
what Mum had asked him to buy.

"Was it sugar?" said the shop lady.

"No," said Alan.

"Tea, then?"

"No," said Alan.

"Maybe it was butter?"

"I don't think so," said Alan.

"But maybe it was."

He went home with some butter.

"Oh Alan," said Mum. "It was bread
I wanted. Never mind,
Janet can go back to the shop."
And Janet went, because she was best
at everything.

Alan went out to play in the garden.
"It isn't fair," he said.
"Janet is always best at everything.
I want to be best at something."

"Maybe you will be," said Mum,
"one day."

Alan sat under the big green bush
at the bottom of the garden.
It was dark and secret.
There were flowers under the bush
that didn't grow in the rest
of the garden.

"Weeds," said Dad. "Can't have them
in my garden."

He dug out the yellow dandelions
and the white daisies
that grew in the lawn
and put them on the rubbish tip.
But Alan liked the little flowers
and tried to make them grow
in the earth under the bush.
Most of the flowers died.

"Why don't they grow?" he asked.

"They have no water," said Mum.

"They need more sunshine," said Dad.

"You are silly," said Janet.
"They're just weeds."

But Alan went on planting them
under the bush
to see what would happen.

One day when he was helping Dad
to tidy the garage
he found an old tin basin
with holes in the bottom.

"Can I have it?" he asked.

Dad gave it to him.

Alan filled the basin with earth.
He planted a yellow dandelion
and two daisies.

He took some water from the kitchen
and put it round the roots
of the flowers. He put the basin
in the sunshine by the back door.

"Very nice," said Mum.

"That looks like a real garden," said Dad.

"You are silly," said Janet.

"They're just weeds."

Alan didn't hear her.

He was looking for more flowers.

On Saturday, Mum and Alan went to
the supermarket. There was a notice of a
flower show in the window.

"Can I take my garden?" asked Alan.

"Why not?" said Mum.

All week Alan worked very hard.

Mum gave him an old fork and spoon
to tidy up his garden.

He found some more flowers

and planted them beside the daisies.
Dad found a big thick patch of
green moss on top of the wall.

"It looks like a lawn," he said.

Alan put the moss
in the middle of the basin
with flowers all around it.
Janet gave him her white china bird
to sit on the lawn.

"Be careful with it," she said.

On Saturday the sun was shining.
Alan got out of bed early
and went to look at his garden.
The pink and white and yellow flowers
were beginning to open
and look up to the sun.
The little white bird
sat on the green moss lawn.
It looked very happy there.

Dad put Alan's garden in the car
and they took it to the Flower Show.
It went on a long table
with some other plants.

Alan looked at the other children's entries.
One girl had a pot of red flowers.
A boy had a plant that ate insects.
There was a very small boy
with a blue and white plate
which had cress growing on it.

The judges came and looked at
the table. They stood and talked
to each other until they had
chosen the winner.
Then one of them smiled

a great big smile at Alan.

His garden had won first prize.

They gave Alan a real garden fork
and a small spade of his own,
and a very big box of sweets.

"I am sure you will be
a very good gardener
when you grow up," said the judge.

"He's very good right now," said Janet.

"Of course he is," said Mum.

"He's the best in the family," said Dad.

Alan was happy. At last
he had found something
that he was best at.

Sandy MacStovie's Monster

Spring had come back to the Highlands.
The deer no longer jumped
in and out of the cottage gardens
to steal food. They had gone back up to the hill
where the new grass was growing again.

The robins no longer stole the cream
off Granny Mac's milk.
Tiger the cat was out and about
now that the sun was warm again.

Down by the loch, Sandy MacStovie
pushed his boat into the water.
He climbed in, pushed the long green oars
into the water and set out

for the island. He rowed round the back
and leaned over the side of the boat.

"Hello," he whispered as loud as
he could. "Are you there?"

At first there was silence,
then a voice bubbled up
from the water.

"No!" it said.

"What do you mean, 'no'?"
whispered Sandy. "You must be there!"

"I'm on strike this year,"
the voice bubbled up again.

"Why?" whispered Sandy,
leaning right over. His nose was nearly
in the water.

"Because . . ." bubbled the voice.

"Because what?" whispered Sandy.
"And come on up and talk to me properly,
you big daft lump."

The water heaved and bubbled.
Sandy's boat bounced about
like a cork. A huge green head
and three humps rose out of the water.

"What's all this about then?"
demanded Sandy. "Look, summer's coming.
The tourists will be here soon
with all their cameras.
They'll be looking for you."
    "I'll tell you something,"
said the monster.
    "What's that?" said Sandy.
"And stop dripping on me."
    "I don't believe in tourists,"
said the monster.

"You don't believe in tourists!"
Sandy was so amazed he forgot
to whisper. "What about all these people
that come to the village?
They come to take photos of
the monster, and leave litter in the road
and park their cars
in Granny Mac's garden."

The monster sniffed.

"They're not real," he said.
"They're just a wee story.
Something you make up so that

we monsters will come up and
look at them."

"Rubbish," said Sandy.

"Well, they said I was just
a made up story," said the monster.
"I heard them. They said I wasn't real.
So I'm taking the hump. In fact
I'm taking THREE humps."

"And you're just the one
to do it!" said Sandy.

The monster tossed his tail.
The splash soaked Sandy from head to foot.

"Come back, you stupid pudding!"
shouted Sandy. It was too late.
The monster had gone back
down into the loch.

The summer came. And the tourists
came too. They left their cars
in Granny Mac's garden
and went off to look for
the monster. But not a nose,
tail or hump was to be seen.

"It's just an old fairy tale,"
they said. They went to look for
a castle with a ghost instead.

Fewer and fewer people came.
Sometimes there were only two or three.
They came and looked and
went away again. They didn't even
buy a postcard in Granny Mac's
sweet shop.

"At home we have a *real* monster,"
said a Japanese tourist to Sandy.
He showed Sandy a Japanese newspaper.
Sandy couldn't read the words,
but he could see the picture.

"Can I have this?" he asked.
That night, as soon as
it was dark, he rowed out

to the island. He leaned over
the side of the boat.

"How are you?" he whispered.
The water bubbled.

"Not bad, not bad," moaned
a sad little voice.

"Come up and look at this,"
said Sandy, holding out the Japanese
newspaper. "You're not the only monster!"

The monster leaned over his shoulder
to look at the newspaper.

"Can't read it," he moaned.

"You can see the picture," said Sandy,
"if you'll stop dripping on it.
There's a real Japanese monster.
It comes up and has photos taken."

"Rubbish," said the monster.
"It's just a TV game."

"Maybe it is," said Sandy,
"but they believe in it.
People haven't seen you for so long
they're saying that you are just
a fairy tale."

"Is that so?" said the monster.
"We'll soon see about that."
With a flick of his tail
he splashed off into the darkness.

Next morning a bus full of tourists
stopped at Granny Mac's shop.
Suddenly a huge green monster shot up
out of the water in front of them.

"Did you see that?" said the tourists.
They fell over each other
trying to take photos.
The monster splashed up and down
the loch. He stood on his tail,
turned circles, made faces at the
tourists and then vanished.

    All that summer Granny Mac's sweet shop
was full of tourists buying postcards.
She did so well that she was
able to open a tea room.
    Sandy took the tourists
out to the island in his boat.
In no time at all he was able
to buy a bigger boat with
an engine and take more tourists.
Hundreds of people came to
look for the monster.

The funny thing was that
no one saw him again that summer.

On some dark nights a strange sound
could be heard. It might have
been a bird. It might have been
a cow sneezing.

Or it might have been a voice
bubbling up from the water.

"Tourists! Humph!"

Loch Ness

Underwater camera and sonar equipment, used for tracking down monsters.

Loch Ness monster 'captured' by Anthony Shiels, 21 May 1977. Do you believe that the monster exists? What kind of animal do you think it is?

The Travelling Shop

There's never a day goes past
but I've got a good story to tell.
You really see life in my job,
and you get a good laugh too.

Who am I? I'm Jim Ferguson, of course.
I drive the travelling shop round
the island. Big Jim the Van, that's
what they call me.

What's a travelling shop? My goodness
– fancy not knowing about the travelling shop!
You climb up and come with me
on my round and I'll tell you
all about it as we go.

You see, the thing is, when you live
out here on the islands, there aren't
many big towns. Most of the people
live in villages and farmhouses
which are a long way from anywhere,
and it's not easy to get to the shops.

It's really difficult if you're old,
or if you have children who
are not at school,
like Alex and Bessie Anne
down at Clach Farm. She's got
the twins – wait till you meet them!

There are many people who
can't get to the shops,
so I take the shop to them.

I've got to deliver a birthday cake
for Shona up at the schoolhouse
this afternoon.
She'll be nine tomorrow,
and she's having a party.
Her mother asked me last week
if I could get a cake iced for her.
You see my wife, that's Mrs Ferguson,

sometimes bakes for people.
She's really good at decorating cakes.

You should see Shona's, it's gorgeous.
It's covered in white icing with
pink shells and pink roses round the top,
and a great big number nine
in pink and silver with
'Happy Birthday Shona' written underneath it.

Now, this is where we have to
watch the road. We turn left
along here and up to the
white cottage on the hill.

Keep your eyes open for the turning.
It's a terrible road up to the cottage,
full of holes and bumps.

Right, here we are, hold on to
your hat now. It's getting worse than ever.
One of these days we'll do this run
and finish up with scrambled eggs
in the back.
And don't suggest they fill in any holes,
or you'll get your nose bitten off.
Old Granny Grumpy the kids call her.

I'll just sound the horn so that
she knows we're coming,
though if she hasn't heard this
van rattling to bits on her road,
she must be stone deaf!

Here she comes out to meet us.
I'll just pull up at the
edge here and go through to the back
to see what she wants.

Are you staying here?
No, you want to come too.
Come on then.

This is the shop part of the van.
Great, isn't it?
See, I've got my scales and the
till for the money here on the
counter, and there are all sorts of
tins and packets on the shelves.
I've got a sack of potatoes and
boxes of vegetables at the front,
and down here there's a box with
all the washing powder and soap.
You can't put them on the shelf beside
the biscuits.

I'll show you round everything later.
Here she comes.

Good morning, Granny. What's it to be
today? Salt, right. Two bags of flour

and sugar. That's it. One cauliflower
and a piece of cheese.
That'll make a nice tea.
And batteries for the radio,
here we are, a packet of four.
Hand me up your basket and I'll
fill it for you.

There you are, that's the lot,
and that's just the right money.
Thank you, Granny. Cheerio.

Right, let's get turned round
and out of here.
What a state! She'll have to
mend her ways, the old lady!

There, that's us, back on
a good road again. We'll go down into
the village now. Watch that pink cottage
at the crossroads just before we get there.
There's a daft dog that jumps out
at anything that goes past,
if the gate's left open.

Look, here it comes now,
stupid thing. Shouting its head off

at one end and wagging its
tail at the other.

Here's the lady waving us down,
better pull in and see what she wants.
You wait there this time.
I think it'll be something quick.

There, I was right. She wanted tea,
baked beans, pot scrubbers and a packet
of soap powder. That sounds like
a tasty meal, doesn't it?

Up to the church now. I've got to
leave extra milk at the hall.
They're having a concert tonight and
from what I hear it's going to be busy.
It's not a very big village,
right enough, but folk come from
all over the island for the concerts.
It's a great night.
I'll be there, with Mrs Ferguson.
In fact she'll have to be there,
she's playing the piano.
One of the stars of the show
is Mrs Ferguson. And that reminds me,

I've got to pick up her dress.
Old Mrs Mac down at Clach, that's
Bessie Anne's neighbour, has made
a new one for her.

   Right, here we are, the church hall.
I'll just hop out and leave the
crate of milk inside the door.

   Out round the shore road now.
Nobody lives round here these days.
It's a wild road in winter, this.
It's bad enough just now.
Look at those waves.
That means there's a gale out at sea.

We go up that road round the cliff top.
There was a van blown off up there,
years ago that was. He was going
just the same run as us with the
travelling shop. No, he didn't go over
the cliff, he stuck in the bushes.
They had to come up and pull him out.
Imagine being stupid enough
to get yourself in a mess like that!

Look, there's Clach Farm down there.
It's the new house at the bottom
of the hill.

Well, at least the twins haven't
burned it down since last week!
I'll sound the horn and let Bessie Anne
know I'm coming. You hop out and
open the gate.
And mind and shut it behind us again.
You've got to keep the animals in . . . aye,
and the twins too! Shhh.

Good morning, Bessie Anne. It's very
quiet this morning. They're both in bed
with measles? Och, that's a pity.
They'll not be at the concert
tonight then? Ah well. . . .
You've quite a shopping list there.
Let's have a look, and we'll
sort it out for you.
I've brought up the wellingtons
for Alec too, size eight, green, and a pair of
pink slippers for yourself.

Here, what's that noise? Someone's
shouting. You go and see and I'll
finish off here.
It'll be the twins, I bet.

They've locked themselves in the
bedroom? Where's Alec, is he up the hill?
I'll get my tool box and
see what we can do.
You wait in the van for me, you don't
want to catch any spots.

  There, back at last. Sorry it took
so long. What a pair!
There's a new form of wildlife
round here, the Greater Spotted Menace,
always goes in pairs.

  It's all right, Bessie Anne, no trouble.
Everything's in your basket.
I'll be back up and
see you again next week.

Just keep that key in your pocket
in future will you?

Come on now. Time for us to get home.
What a morning!
We'll go back round the cliff road –
it's quicker. My, it's a grand view from
up here, you can see right down the coast.

There are caravans and tents down there
in the summer, but it's a bit early
in the season yet.

  We do quite well with the holidaymakers.
They always buy bread and milk
and eggs and things like that.

  We haven't forgotten something, have we?
The dress! You're right.
Mrs Ferguson will murder me
if I go back without it.
The twins made me forget all about it.
We'll just have to go back down to
Mrs Mac's and collect it.

  We'll have to turn round up here.
It's all right, we won't need to
go near the cliff edge.
Just keep an eye out
at the back and I'll pull round
as far as I can.
Don't worry, I know it's a long way down.
I'll be careful. Keep a look out
at the back there.
I'm all right so far.

If I go back a bit more
I can pull right round in one.
Oh no!

It's no use shoving, the van's
too heavy. The back wheel's just sinking
further in. Try again, there's
an old sack in the back,
we'll put it under the wheel.
Right, stand back, we're off.
No, we're not.

That's all we need, here's some
daft sheep coming down to see
what's going on.
They're looking for a sandwich.
The campers feed them in the summer.
Go on! Shoo!

I'll start the engine again.
Come on, one more shove.
Ready, one-two-three. Push!
Not a thing.
Well, there's only one thing to do.
We'll walk back down to Clach Farm.
Alex will be down off the hill
soon and he can come up
with the tractor and pull us out.
While we're waiting for him
I'll walk over and collect the dress
from Mrs Mac, and maybe Bessie Anne
will give us a cup of tea.
One thing about this job, I did
tell you, it's never dull.
You coming?

Greta's Shetland Shawl

When you were a baby, did you have
a soft woollen shawl?
Perhaps you know a baby
who has a shawl like that.
If you open it out you will see
that the fine wool makes patterns.
Some of them are like the frost
on a window in winter.
Others are like the silver spiders' webs
that you see in summer time.

Shawls like these first came from
the Shetland Islands, far out in
the wild sea to the north of Scotland.
The women of the islands used to
sit and knit by the fire
during the winter nights.
As they did their knitting
they told stories.
This was one of them.

Many years ago there was a child
called Greta. She lived with her mother
in a cottage by the beach.
Greta's father had been a fisherman,
but now he was dead. Greta's mother
worked hard all day in the little garden.
She tried to grow enough food
for them to eat.
Greta worked in the house,
spinning the wool from their sheep
so that her mother could sell it
in the market.
    One cold day, while her mother was

in the village, Greta sat by the
window spinning. Sea spray, blown by
the gales of winter,
washed over the little cottage.
As Greta watched the ribbons of water
run down the glass,
she suddenly saw something else.

Up in the dark corner
at the top of the window
a large spider was starting
to spin his web. He swung down
on a long thread to the bottom corner.
He climbed to the top again and
made threads to the other corners.
At last the little window
was filled with a fine silver star.

Then the spider really set to work.
In and out, round and round he went,
faster than the dancers at a wedding.
He filled the window with a curtain
of the finest lace.

Greta forgot her spinning-wheel.
She stared in wonder.

A light seemed to shine through
the little window.
The spider was slowly changing into
a tiny man with a round rosy face.
He lifted his hat, and his hair was like
the silver threads of the web.

"Good day to you," he said.
"My work is to your liking?"

Greta nodded. She was afraid to whisper
in case she blew away the beautiful web.

"Look well," said the tiny man,
"and you will learn how it is done."

He wove in and out through the web.
He went slowly, so that Greta
could see how the patterns were made.

As she watched, she saw her mother
coming home along the beach.
She ran to the door.

"Come quickly," she called. "Come and
see what the little man has
shown me." But by the time Greta's mother
came in, the little man had vanished.

"It's only a spider making a web,"
she laughed. "You must have been dreaming.
I'll dust it in the morning."

"Oh, no," said Greta. "We must
leave it!" So they left it.

That night Greta lay in bed
thinking of the little man
and his beautiful web.

In the morning she took the finest,
whitest wool from the basket
and set to work.
She carded the wool,
brushing out all the knots.
She started to spin,
but the wool was too thick.
She tried again.

This time the wool was
too thin and it broke.
Again and again she tried.

At last, at the end of a week
and a day, she had spun
a ball of wool. It was fine and
white, like the spider's web.

Greta took a pair of
knitting pins of the best
apple wood, smooth as a
sea pebble, and started
to knit her wool.

She sat by the window.
From time to time she stopped to look at the web
which the little man had made.

She knitted through long winter days
when the web sparkled with frost.

She knitted during dark nights
when it shone in the candlelight.

She knitted on bright spring mornings
when the web twinkled in the sunlight.

She knitted a wonderful web of
fine white wool.

Her mother told the women
in the village, and they came to sit
and watch her work.
Word spread far and wide
through the islands.
At last it came to the ears of the
Princess of the North.
She was soon to be married
to the King of Norway.

The princess went to the island
where Greta lived so that she might
see this wonder for herself.

She lifted the fine lace that Greta
had knitted. It floated round her
like sea mist on a summer morning.

"I'd like this for my wedding,
Greta," she whispered. "Would you
sell it to me for a piece of gold?"

"I will not sell it," said Greta.
"But give me your ring."

"But that's the ring that
the King of Norway himself gave me,"
said the princess.

"Give it to me," said Greta.
The princess took off the little
golden ring and gave it to her.

Greta held up the ring. Then,
very slowly and carefully,
she pulled the knitting through the ring.
The wool was so fine and
the stitches so tiny that it
slid easily through the ring.

"There," said Greta. "It's fit
for a princess. I won't

sell it to you, I'll
give it to you as a gift
for your wedding."

The princess was so happy that
she put a bag of gold pieces
on the table.

"It's yours," she said. "I won't
pay you. I'll give it as a gift."

The princess wore the lace shawl
for her wedding. And all who saw her
talked of nothing else.

When her first son was born,
the princess wrapped him gently in
Greta's wonderful shawl.

Greta lived long and happily in
the little cottage by the beach.
She taught the other women of the islands
how to knit, as the little man
had shown her. These women passed on
the gift to their children in turn.
Today, babies everywhere are still wrapped
in the warmth and love
of Greta's Shetland shawl.

The Mountain Rescue

Sergeant Donnie Maclean
stood at the open door
of the police station.
The road was quiet and empty.
Here and there a light shone
from the windows of the village houses.

"Tea's ready, Donnie!" Marie, his wife,
called from the kitchen.
The village police station
was also their home.

Donnie took a last look around.
The little houses looked warm and cosy
in the spring evening.
Here and there clumps of yellow daffodils
shone brightly in the gardens.

Behind the houses,
and high above them all,
the mountains were blue and gold
in the setting sun.
Most of the snow had melted now.
Only on the high slopes
were there still white patches.

"They look like hankies
tucked in a pocket," said Marie.

Donnie laughed.

"They'll be wet soon," he said.
He closed the door
and followed her through
to the bright living-room
where tea was set on the table.
The wind rose, shaking the bushes
in the garden as they ate.
Hailstones rattled the window.

"It'll be a wild night," said Donnie.
"I'm glad I'm not going out in it."

"Such a pity, after the lovely day
it has been," said Marie.
She poured last cups of tea

for them both and took the plates
through to the kitchen.
Just then the telephone rang.

"If that's the doctor
wanting me to go down
and play darts with him again,
tell him I'm not coming,"
said Donnie. "He's too good for me!"

"It isn't the doctor,"
Marie called through. "It's Jimmy,
the warden up at the Youth Hostel.
There's someone missing.
He wants to talk to you."

Donnie sighed.

"I knew it was too good
to last," he said.

Jimmy, the warden, was worried.
A young man from Edinburgh
had been at the hostel
for four days now. Each day
he had gone out
hill-walking on his own.
He seemed to know

what he was doing, Jimmy said.
He had maps and a compass.
He always wore warm clothes
and good strong boots.
He always packed a bag
with sandwiches and two flasks,
one of tea and one of soup,
to take with him.

"He's maybe just stopped to shelter
from the storm," said Donnie.
The hailstones were still
rattling on the glass.

"I don't think so," said Jimmy.
"He's always been back
by five o'clock at the latest.
Today he said he would be early
because he's leaving in the morning."

Donnie looked at his watch.
It was half-past eight.

"Give him another hour or two,"
he said, "and then we'll decide
what to do."

At ten o'clock he pulled on
his big anorak and drove
up the hill to the Youth Hostel.
The rain was turning to sleet,
and a high wind
tossed the tops of the trees.
Jimmy was waiting by the door.

"There's no sign of him," he shouted.

"Where was he going?" asked Donnie,
pulling out a map.

"Up the Ben." Jimmy pointed
to the highest peak.
"He said it looked like

an easy climb from here."

"He'll maybe not
be thinking that now," said Donnie.
"I'd better get the team out."

Twenty minutes later five men met
at the police station.
The doctor and Big Jock the plumber
were still arguing about darts.
Donnie had found them in the local pub.

Pete, who owned the village shop,
grumbled as he pulled on
his climbing boots.

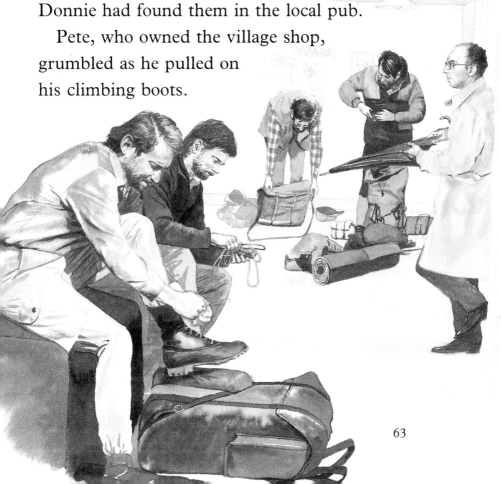

"That's the third time I've tried
to see that film on television,
and I'm missing the end again.
I'll never know what happened."

"Who is it and what happened?"
asked Archie, stamping in out of the rain.

He was the oldest member of the team,
and a local school teacher.
He spent the long summer holidays
walking and climbing,
and had grown up among the hills.
He knew every inch of the Ben,
and had climbed it in sun and snow.
He was a good man to have
on a Mountain Rescue Team.

"He was climbing the Ben," said Donnie,
spreading the map across the table.
"Going up from the Youth Hostel."

"He'll likely be somewhere
on the west face then," said Archie.
"It'll be difficult
to get out of the wind
there tonight."

They sorted out torches,
whistles and food, and helped
each other on with their backpacks.
Jock carried the light silver pipes
that screwed together
to make a stretcher.
Donnie carried the radio.
He had called in
one of his men to stay by
the radio in the police station.

"We'll let you know what we're doing
once we get up," he said.
"It'll take an hour or two.
We'll maybe find him sheltering
in one of the shepherds' huts."
But the huts were empty and unused.

The rescue team climbed on,
checking the gullies and caves
where a climber might have taken shelter.
They called and whistled,
working their way slowly round the mountain.
But there was no answer.
The night wore on, cold and wet.
The men grew tired, and had to
stop more often for a rest.

They came together
in the first grey light of
early morning on the high
slopes of the Ben.
Beneath them, the village
with the river and the
pale ribbon of road lay spread out
like a huge map.

The wind was icy and rain stung their faces.
Pete stamped his feet.

"I hope he's well wrapped up," he said,
"wherever he is."

"We're not going to find him
like this," said Donnie.
"I think we need some help."

The doctor nodded.

"It's light enough
for a helicopter now," he said.
"But what about the wind?"

"Leave that to them," said Archie.
"They'll do their best.
Let's have some breakfast."

Donnie sent a radio message
down to the village.
As they ate, the message was passed on
from the police to the Rescue Centre.
From the Rescue Centre a call went out
to a cold windswept airfield.
Four young men pulled themselves
out of warm beds and climbed
into flying suits.

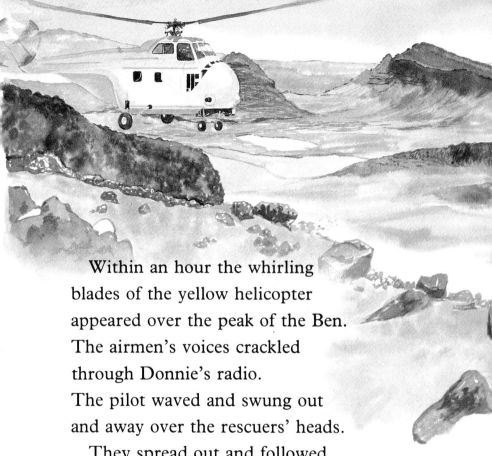

Within an hour the whirling
blades of the yellow helicopter
appeared over the peak of the Ben.
The airmen's voices crackled
through Donnie's radio.
The pilot waved and swung out
and away over the rescuers' heads.

They spread out and followed
the helicopter. It climbed slowly towards
the top of the Ben. Now and then
it vanished in a patch of cloud.
A gust of wind blew down,
bringing icy rain with it.
The men turned their faces away,
and climbed on.

Suddenly the radio crackled.

"Say that again!" shouted Donnie.
The others gathered round him.

"Got him!" the pilot's voice came back.
"He's up by the waterfall,
near the top. He's wearing a red
anorak and green backpack."

"Ask if he looks all right,"
the doctor shouted in Donnie's ear.

"He's waving," said the pilot.
"Looks pleased to see us!

But he can't move. It looks as if
there's been a rock slide.
There's a lot of water
coming down the falls."

"Can you lift him
out of there?" asked Donnie.

"No!" the pilot shouted back.
"Can't get near him.
He's tucked in under a rock.
There's nowhere to land.
We can't get close enough
to swing a man in on a rope.
You'll have to get him out yourself.
We'll stand by above
so that you know where he is."

"Come on!" said the doctor.
"Let's get him out of there fast.
He must be pretty cold by now."
He and Jock set off up the hillside.

"There's a quicker way round
than that," said Archie, pointing across
the rocks. Pete and the others
turned to follow him.

"We're on our way," shouted Donnie
into the radio.
"See you at the top."
The pilot waved. The helicopter
turned away up the mountain.
Far below, he could see
the tiny figures of the Mountain
Rescue Team, setting out to bring home
one very wet and very tired climber.

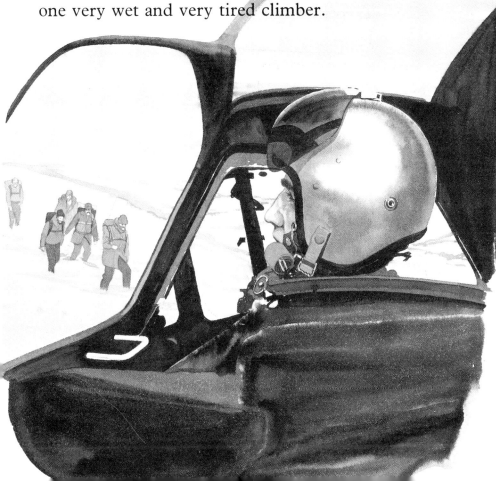

Sea King helicopter doing a winch lift in Glencoe. The winch wire is almost 100 metres long. Describe how you would feel if you had to be rescued like this.

Hallowe'en

15 Market Street,
Drumglass.
10th November

Dear Aunt Helen,

Thank you for your letter from Paris last month.

Thank you too for all the stamps you sent me. It must be fun working in an office where you get letters from all over the world.

I am sticking them in a book. All the flower stamps go on one page, then all the animals on the next. I think the page of Christmas stamps is the best.

It will soon be time for Christmas again. Shall I tell you what I would like?
Mum has just read this bit and she says to make it something small, and not heavy.

John says can he have lots of
five pound notes, then, please?

Will I tell you what we
have been doing? Well, first of all
there is school. That's boring,
so that's all I can tell you
about it. My friend Gillian has chickenpox
so I have been told not to visit her
in case I catch it too.
So that's what I have
not been doing. That's boring too.

The best thing we did was Hallowe'en.
That was before Gillian had chickenpox,
we went out together.
I can tell you all about that.
Mum says that you used to dress up
and go out on Hallowe'en
when you were my age,
so maybe you still remember about it.

In the middle of October
Gillian and I decided we were going to
dress up and go out on Hallowe'en
night this year. She decided to be

a paintbox, because painting is her
best thing at school.
I wanted to be a gypsy.

   We made a paintbox costume out of
a big cardboard box from the supermarket.
First of all we cut a hole
in the top so that Gillian
could stand inside and put her head
out at the top. Then we made holes
for her arms in the sides.

   Dad let us paint it with some
old white paint out in the garage.
He said the floor needed a bit of
paint anyway. It was a bit messy.

When it was dry we took
some of Gillian's poster paints and
made squares of colour on the front.
It was red, green, blue and yellow,
just like a real paintbox.
Gillian tried to make purple with the
red and blue but it looked
like mud, so we painted black over it.

I am sending you a picture of Gillian
wearing her paintbox. She looked funny,
and had to stand up all the time.

She carried a mop for a paintbrush.

My costume was lovely. I wore
the red skirt with the big frill
that we got from Alison's Mum.
It is too small for Alison now,
and she gave it to me for next summer.
It is really too big for me
just now, but it was good for
being a gypsy in.
I had a white blouse, with
Mum's blue waistcoat.
She let me have
the red scarf with roses on it
to tie round my hair.
Gillian's Mum has a lovely silver scarf
and she tied it round the middle.
It was really to hold the skirt up,
but it looked very pretty.
I wanted to have Mum's earrings
but she said that I might lose them,
so we made some out of cardboard.
I covered them with silver paper
and tied them on with bits of wool.

After that I had to make my
face brown. Mum let me use some
of the suntan cream she had
during the summer.
I had red lipstick and green colour
on my eyes. John said I looked like
a pop star on television.
I didn't look like me, anyway.

We waited until after tea-time
before we went out. It was really dark,
but we had a big torch.
It really belonged to Gillian's brother.
He said she could use it if she
paid him for half of a new battery.

John made us a big turnip lantern.
Really, I think he only did it
because he wanted to try out
his new penknife. He cut out
all the inside and cut a face
with little holes for the eyes and a
big smiling mouth. We put a candle
inside and Dad lit it for us.
Here is a drawing of it.

Do you think I'm getting quite good
at drawing? I think I might be
an artist when I leave school.

We went next door to Mrs White's.
When she came to the door
we both shouted,
"Can we have our Hallowe'en?"
She said she didn't know me
at all with the make-up on.
She knew Gillian though,
because she giggles a lot.

I sang two pop songs and Gillian
told some jokes, but she got
in a muddle with the end of them
and started to giggle so much
that nobody could understand them.

Mrs White gave us each
an apple and some peanuts and
Mr White gave us each
ten pence, so that was quite good.

When we got out again
Gillian tried to tell the jokes
to me, but she still couldn't remember
the end of them so we decided
to sing the pop songs together.

We went to quite a lot of
houses and collected lots more

apples and nuts and some more
money and a packet of peppermints.

It was windy and the candle in
the turnip lantern blew out.
I thought it was a good thing really
because it had a horrible smell,
and the top had gone all black inside.

When we got home Mum made us both
a cup of cocoa and we ate
some of the peppermints and
an apple each. We counted out
all the money, so that we both
had the same. I gave ten pence

to John because he made the
turnip lantern, and Gillian saved
ten pence for her brother
to help pay for his torch battery.
They both said it wasn't enough.
We said if they wanted more
they should do their own singing.

It was a very good Hallowe'en.
Do the children in France dress up
and go out for Hallowe'en like that?

Love,
Catriona

Hamish and the Big Wind

A long time ago an old woman
and her son Hamish
lived on a farm.
They kept one cow, two pigs, six hens,
and a black and white dog.

Hamish worked very hard.
He looked after the animals,
and in the summer he grew vegetables
in the garden and made hay
in the fields.

The farm was always clean and tidy.
People used to say that Hamish's
big round haystacks were the best
in the whole of Scotland.

And so they were, until the night
of the Big Wind.

Hamish had finished working
for the day. He sat in front of
the fire, warming his toes.
He sang a song to himself
and listened to the fire crackling
and potatoes bubbling in the big pot.
Everything was quiet.

Suddenly there was a crash
and a whoosh. A Big Wind
howled down the chimney.
It shook the windows and doors
until they rattled,
then blew out into the farmyard.
Hamish pulled on his boots and
ran outside.

What a mess!

The Big Wind had stormed round
the farm, knocking down the gate.
The door of the barn
had been blown open.
Inside, the animals were
making a great noise.
The cow mooed, and stamped around.
The pigs grunted and snorted.
The hens flapped around,
clucking to each other.

"Where is it? Where did it go?
What was it?"

Worst of all, Hamish's two
big round haystacks
had been blown right away.

"What a dreadful mess!" said Hamish.
He set to work to tidy up.
When he had finished, he went to
his mother.

"The Big Wind has blown off with
my two haystacks," he said.
"I'm going to follow it and
bring them back."

His mother took down a
strong leather bag that hung on a peg
behind the door.

"If you are going," she said,
"you'll need to take some food with you."

She put some bread and cheese
into the bag and tied it
tightly round the top with a rope.

Hamish took the bag and said goodbye.
He set off down the hill,
following the Big Wind.
He walked for miles, and had eaten

most of the cheese and bread,
when he came to a farm.

"Have you seen the Big Wind
pass this way?" Hamish asked.

"I have indeed," said the farmer.
"He came over here last night
and blew away with the roof of
my cowshed and my best wheelbarrow."

"Which way did he go?" asked Hamish,
"because he blew away with
my two big round haystacks.
I'm going to bring them back.
I'll try to find the roof
of your cowshed and the
wheelbarrow as well."

"He went up the hill and over
the moor," said the farmer.
"But it's a long cold road.
Stop and have some food first."
Hamish sat down with the farmer
for a meal. When he had finished,
the farmer filled his leather bag
with the rest of the cold meat
and another bit of bread.
Hamish said goodbye and set off
on the road up the hill.

He walked and walked. After two days
he came to a little village by
the sea. On the cliff top
above the village stood a huge
grey castle. The windows looked out across
the sea to a little island.

Hamish asked the people of the village
if they had seen the Big Wind.

"We have indeed," said an old woman.
"He came blowing through here
just last night.
But you ask up at the king's castle.
Someone there will tell you
about the Big Wind."

90

"I didn't know there was
a king here," said Hamish.

"Of course there is," said the
old woman. "And he's very angry
with the Big Wind. They say
the king will give a fine prize
to the man who can catch him."

"That's good news," said Hamish,
"for I am that man."

The king and his family
were at dinner when Hamish reached
the castle. When the king heard
about Hamish he asked him to
sit down and join them.

"We've all tried to catch
the Big Wind," he said,
"but it's no use. Do you think
you can do it?"

"Of course I can," said Hamish.

"If you do," said the king, "I'll
give you a bag of gold,
and you can have one of my
daughters to be your wife."

Hamish looked at the king's daughters.
There were six of them.
Five were tall and thin,
with fair hair and blue eyes.
The sixth was small and plump,
with red hair and green eyes.
Hamish smiled at her.
She giggled, went pink,
and shook her red curly hair.

    "That's Mirren," said the king.
"She's the youngest one."

"And the prettiest," said Hamish.
"She's the one I will marry.
Now, where is this Big Wind?"

The king led him over to the window.

"Do you see that island?"
He pointed to the little island
across the sea. "The Big Wind
lives in an old castle
out there. What you must do is
go and catch him. But be careful."

"Leave it to me," said Hamish.

The king lent him a small
brown boat. He also tried to give him
a sword and a helmet.

"No," said Hamish. "There is
only one other thing I need."

The only thing he took with him
was the leather bag that his mother
had given him, with the strong
rope to tie round the top.

When he reached the island
Hamish was amazed at the sight.
He pulled the little boat up

on to the beach and looked around.
He saw his two big round haystacks,
the cowshed roof, and the farmer's
best wheelbarrow. There was also some washing
that had been blown from a line,
and many other things as well.
Hamish had started to load them
into the boat, when the Big Wind
came whistling up.

"Oooooo-hoooo!" he roared. "And where
do you think you're going with these?"

"I'm taking them back where they belong,"
said Hamish.

"Oooooo-hoooo you're not,"
roared the Big Wind.

"Try and stop me," shouted Hamish.

The Big Wind whirled round.
He didn't like Hamish being cheeky
to him. He stormed down to try and
catch him. Hamish was too quick.
He jumped in behind an old
stone pillar. Then he popped his
head out and shouted at the Big Wind.

"You can't catch me
      For a wee bawbee!"
The Big Wind roared in fury.
That started a racing and chasing
round the castle. Hamish jumped
in and out of doors and windows,
and up and down the stairs.
The Big Wind stormed behind, trying
to catch him.

"Stand still for a minute," he howled.

Hamish stuck out his tongue.

"You can't catch me,
      For a wee bawbee!"
The Big Wind screamed louder than ever.
Hamish climbed quickly up the huge chimney
over the empty fireplace.

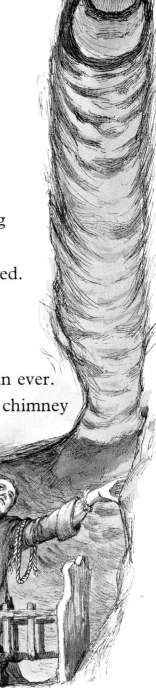

The Big Wind screamed up after him.

"Ooooo-hooooo," he howled. "Just wait
till I catch you!"

Hamish climbed out at the top
of the chimney, and quick as a flash
opened his big leather bag over it.

"Ooooo-hooooo," roared the Big Wind.
He blew straight up into the
big leather bag. Hamish tied
the strong bit of rope
round the top, with three knots,
and stuffed the bag back into the chimney.

It is still there to this day,
and if you visit that island
you can hear the Big Wind
howling to be let out of the chimney.

Hamish took his two big round haystacks
and went back to the king.
When he told the story about
the Big Wind, people came from
every corner of Scotland to find
the things that the Big Wind
had stolen from them.

And what about the king's youngest daughter
Mirren, who giggled and shook her red curls?
She and Hamish were married,
and there was a great feast at the castle
that went on for days and days.
The king wanted Hamish to stay there,
and for a while he did.

But at last he began to miss
his farm with the one cow,
two pigs, six hens and the
black and white dog.
So one fine morning Hamish and Mirren
packed their bags and set off
across the hills to the little cottage,
where they lived happily ever after.

Tam Lin

O I forbid you maidens a',
  That wear gowd in your hair,
To come or gae by Carterhaugh,
  For young Tam Lin is there.

Janet put down her sewing
and gazed across the garden
to the green woods of Carterhaugh.
  The woods and much of the
country around belonged to her father.
She could ride and hunt
as far as the eye could see
and still be on her father's land.
But to the woods of Carterhaugh
she knew she must never go.
  Some people said that Carterhaugh was haunted.
  "They say it belongs to
the Little Folk!" some of them said.
"We dare not go there
for fear of what might happen."
  "Carterhaugh is not haunted," said others.
"It is enchanted."

Janet had ridden by the woods
and had seen how in the spring
the early primroses shone like
yellow stars among the grass.
In Carterhaugh the new green leaves of
summer first appeared. They stayed long after
all the trees in her father's garden
were bare and brown. Janet longed
to walk in the deep green shade
of these magic woods.
The more she was told that she
must not, the more she wanted to go.

At last, one summer evening,
she could bear it no longer.
She opened the gate in the
high garden wall, lifted her long green
skirts, and ran down the hot dusty road.
The woods lay ahead,
cool and dark in the setting sun.

Above her head a bird sang a
sweet song. She stepped slowly
across the carpet of moss,
deeper into the shadow of the trees.
The wild flowers seemed to turn
their faces to watch as she passed.
A rose bush grew across the path
and Janet reached up to pick
one of the pale pink flowers.

"Who gave you leave, lady,
to steal from my woods?"

She whirled round. Behind her stood
a tall dark young man.
He was finely dressed in
gold and green.

"The woods are mine, sir," she said.
"This land belongs to my father.
And who are you?"

"Carterhaugh belongs to the Little People,
the Fairy Folk," he said.
"And I, Tam Lin,
must protect it for them."

"Are you one of the Fairy Folk?"
Janet whispered. And indeed there did seem
something strange about the young man
as he stood by her side
in the fading light.

"That I am," he smiled
and made a low bow.
"But I was not always so.
Come with me, fair Janet,
for I know your name.
I will show you flowers
more beautiful than these!"

They walked deeper into the woods
and talked for what seemed many hours.
But always the evening light
was the same among the trees.

It was neither light nor dark.

"I must leave," she said at last.
"My father will be searching for me.
I have been away a long time."

"Not so long," laughed Tam Lin.
"Not so long."

And indeed, when Janet returned
to her father's garden it was
as if she had never been away.
The time in the enchanted woods
had passed in the wink of an eye,
and no one had even noticed
that she had gone.

★　　★　　★　　★　　★

After that, she thought more and more
of Tam Lin. During the long days
of summer she walked in the garden
trying to forget the enchanted woods.
But she could think of nothing
but the strange young man.
Thinking of him she grew to
love him. She became thin and pale.

At last she knew that she must
return to Carterhaugh and tell
Tam Lin of her love.

By this time the cold winds of October
had swept through the garden
and stripped the trees.
The flowers had fallen,
their bright petals grey and dead.

Janet ran to the woods,
her feet crunching on the fallen leaves.
And there, by the wild rose bush,
as though waiting for her,
stood Tam Lin.

"Let me stay with you," she begged.
"Let me live by your side."

"You cannot," he said.
"The Fairy Folk would not let you.
But Janet, if you love me enough
I can become a human again.
And I will be your own true husband."

"Tell me then. Tell me
how I can help you," begged Janet.

Tam Lin told her of the days

when he had been a young man
like any other.
He had not listened to
the words of warning about Carterhaugh,
and had gone riding there.
A deep sleep had come over him
in the woods, and he had awakened
to find himself a prisoner of the Fairies.

"The Queen of the Fairies
has taken me to be
her own knight," he said.
"I am under their magic
and must obey their commands."

Janet wept to hear this.

"There is only one day," he said,
taking her hands, "when you can
save me. Tomorrow is Hallowe'en,
when the Fairy Folk will ride
to Miles Cross. I will be with them.
If you wish to save me
you must be waiting there.
But you need to be brave
and have no fear,

whatever may happen."

"That I will," she said,
"for I love you dearly."

"Then here is what you must do,"
said Tam Lin. "There will be
many of us. But you must wait
for the milk-white horse
on which I ride. When you see me,
pull me down and hold me
in your arms. The Queen of the
Fairies will be angry. She will try
everything in her power to free me.
First she will turn me into a lizard,
then into a snake.
But hold fast, fair Janet. Hold fast!"

"That I will," promised Janet.

"She will then turn me into
a wild deer," said Tam Lin.
"And then at last into an iron,
hot from the fire.
But hold fast, Janet, and
nothing will hurt you."

"And then you will be mine?" she asked.

"For ever and a day, fair Janet,"
he promised. "For ever and a day."

So it happened as Tam Lin had said.
The next night Janet put on a
warm cloak, crept out of the house
and ran to Miles Cross.

About the midnight hour she heard
the ring of bells on bridles
as the Fairy Folk came down the hill.
Even in the dark
Janet could see by the light of
their far-off lanterns.

In front of them all
rode the Queen herself. From head to foot
she glowed silver-green in the dark night.
Janet stared in wonder
as she passed with all her strange company.
But then came a milk-white horse
with her own Tam Lin.

She jumped forward
and pulled him from the horse.
Around her the fairies
screeched and screamed.

With a great flash, Tam Lin turned
from a man to small green lizard
wriggling in her hands.
But still she held fast.

The lizard became a snake
twisting and winding around her arms.
But still she held him to her.

The snake became a wild deer,
tossing and leaping.

Her hands were locked
around his neck.

And then suddenly the deer fell at her
feet, as a lump of hot glowing iron.
But still Janet thought nothing of herself,
only of her true Tam Lin.
She held on.

"You have stolen the fairest knight
in all my company!" screamed the Fairy Queen.
Her voice was like an icy wind of winter.
"You will not have him," shouted Janet,
still holding the hot iron.
"I have broken your spell,
because I love him.
I am not afraid of you."

As she spoke, the Fairy Folk
whirled around her head
like a great storm of green light.
There came an uncanny scream,
fading across the hills.
The stars above them twinkled
in the still dark night.

They were gone. Janet held Tam Lin,
her own true love, in her arms.

Annie's Picnic

Annie wriggled her toes in the dust.
It had been a hot dry summer.
In the quiet afternoon air
she could hear her father whistle
to the dog. Annie's two brothers
were with him, helping to bring
the sheep down from the hill.
Behind her, Mum rubbed and scrubbed
at the washing in the old tub
by the back door.

In the kitchen, the baby began to cry.
Mum stood up and stretched her back.

"See to him lass, will you?" she said,
and went back to scrubbing Annie's
white pinafore.

It was dark in the kitchen
after the sunshine outside.
The baby lay in his basket,
kicking and yelling. He was trying to
push his little round fist into
his mouth. Annie knew that his

new teeth were hurting him.
She carried him out into the yard.

"Can I take him for a walk
up the hill?" she asked.

"Aye," said her mother, "but don't be
late getting back. Mind you don't miss
your tea again."

"I'll mind," Annie laughed. She lifted
the baby out of his basket
and set off up the hill.
The heather felt rough under her bare feet.
It felt better than the black boots
that she had to wear in winter.
Annie hated them. She hated the black
woollen stockings that made her legs itch.
She hated the thick heavy petticoats
she had to wear. Most of all she hated
being a girl. She wanted to be a boy
and work up on the hill
with her father. But she had to
stay and help her mother to cook
and wash and look after the baby.

Annie climbed up the hill

beside the burn. Sometimes she walked
on the grass. Sometimes she paddled
in the water. It was cold and clear
and brown.

On and on she climbed. The only sounds
she could hear were the sheep, and
high above, a little bird sang a song
that spread out over the moor.
A breeze blew over the hill,
lifting her hair.

She reached the top of the hill
and started to run down the other side,
jumping and skipping over the clumps of
grass. The baby laughed in her ear.

Suddenly she stopped.

At the bottom of the hill, by the burn,
there were ponies and people.
A tall man in a kilt
was holding one of the ponies.
Two ladies were taking something
from a basket on its back.

A small plump lady in a dark dress
and bonnet sat on a stone, watching.
Looking up, she saw Annie and the baby
and waved to her to come down.
Annie stood, afraid to go and
afraid to run back over the hill.
The man in the kilt came up to her.

"There's nothing to be afraid of, lass,"
he said. "The fine lady just wants a word
with you."

Hugging the baby tightly to her
she followed him down the hill to where
the little old lady sat.

"What's your name, girl?" asked
the old lady.

"Annie, please ma'am," said Annie.

"And is this your brother, Annie?"

asked the old lady. "He seems
very heavy for you to carry."

Annie put the baby down on
the grass. He pushed his hand
into his mouth and started
to cry again. The little old lady smiled
and her bright blue eyes twinkled.

"I expect he may be hungry," she said.
"Let us see what we can do about it."

The others brought over the large basket
and opened it. Annie's eyes grew wide.

There were cups and saucers and plates,
real china ones. The old lady
lifted out a parcel wrapped in
a white cloth, opened it and
took out a sandwich.
It was small and fine. Annie had
never seen anything like it before.
The baby took it
and stopped crying.

They gave Annie a plate and
filled it with sandwiches.
Just as she thought that
she couldn't eat another thing
the old lady smiled again.

"Cake," she said, "and
this one is my favourite!"

She opened another parcel and gave Annie
a slice of dark brown cake.
It tasted sweet and sticky.

"Chocolate," said the old lady,
nibbling her slice. "Quite delicious."

After tea they sat and talked.
The old lady asked Annie about her home.

Annie told her about her father and
brothers and the sheep.

"I didn't want to be a lass," she said.
"I'd like fine to be a boy
and work on the hill with my father."

The old lady smiled.

"There's nothing wrong with
being a lass," she said.
"You have a fine place to live and
these lovely hills around Balmoral for
your home. I wish I had been
a lass like you. I would like
to live like your Mamma, with
my fine husband and family round me
at the end of the day,
but I cannot."

Her smile was sad, and sweet.

"Go home with you now," she said.
"They will be looking for you and
worried about the baby."

They wrapped a piece of the
chocolate cake in a cloth and
gave it to Annie. The man

in the kilt walked back with her,
and on the way they met her father
and brothers out looking for her.

Annie told them at home about the
old lady and gave them the cake.
Her mother unwrapped it and looked at
the cloth in amazement. There was a crown
and some initials sewn in one corner.

"Mercy on us!" she gasped, sitting down
with a thump. "Here we've been,
worrying about our wee Annie,
and she's been out having tea
with Queen Victoria herself!"

Balmoral Castle

Highland Wildlife

Have you ever climbed to the top
of a hill in the country
and then listened to
the sounds around you?
What can you hear?
   Far off in the distance there is
the bleat of a sheep.
High above your head a bird sings.
Stand still and listen very carefully.
In the long grass at your feet,
you can hear the crick, crick, crick
of a grasshopper.

They are all small animals,
making quiet, peaceful sounds.
But Scotland was not always like that.

Thousands of years ago there were
great storms. Ice and snow
covered the whole country.
For many years neither people nor animals
could live there.
But at long last the weather
began to change.

Spring came slowly. The ice
began to break up. As it melted
the ice turned into gushing rivers
and waterfalls. The water moved rocks
to make valleys and mountains.

As the snow melted and the sun
came back to the land,
the grey rocky country became green.
Here and there a patch of moss
grew on the rock.
Seeds were blown on the wind.
First grass and then trees
took root and began to spread.

Soon the country was covered
with huge forests.

Birds and animals came north
to this new, rich land.
They were looking for food
and for a place to rear their young.

Deer skipped through the trees.
Wolves and foxes followed them.
Wild cattle, rather like Highland cattle
with huge, wicked horns,
wandered about the hillsides
eating the grass.

Hawks and eagles swooped high overhead.
They were hunting hares and rabbits,
which had returned to live
in the valleys below.

Brown bears lived with their cubs
in rocky caves along the river banks.
They hunted for fish
in the freezing water
that poured down
from the snow-capped mountains.

The country was rich and green.

The animals went
further and further north
as the snows melted.

It must have seemed a wonderful place
to the first people
who came hunting for food.
They were also hunting for skins
to protect themselves and their families
from the cold.

They were looking for caves
where they could live in safety.

There were many wild animals
in the forests at night.
If people built huge fires by their caves,
no animals would dare
to come near the flames.
And so the hunters
kept themselves warm and safe.

They began to live together,
at first just in families.
Then groups of families
living near each other
became tribes. They shared
food and fires.
They felt safer
if they cleared away the trees
around their caves
and used the wood to build fences.
Inside the fences they grew
a few plants for food.
They caught and kept a few animals.
They became farmers instead of hunters.

Over many years most of the forests
were cut down. More people came,

so more land was needed
to grow food for them.
Wild animals were driven from their homes,
and many died. Bears and wolves
were hunted until there were none left.
Deer ran from the shelter of
the trees to the high hillsides.

Today you can find places in Scotland
where there are no trees.
The only sounds you will hear
are from sheep put there by a farmer,
insects in the long grass,
or the lonely calls of a
bird on the wing.

You can still see
the kind of creatures
which once lived in the wild,
if you go to a wildlife park
or a zoo where they are
fed and cared for.

Some animals and birds are
protected by law, such as ospreys
and sea eagles.

Slowly Scottish wildlife is coming back.
People try to help
the creatures that are left,
instead of hunting and killing them.
Trees are being planted
to cover the bare hillsides.
Animals and birds will live again
in the land that
man took away from them.

Some native animals, such as this mountain goat and wildcat, can still be found in parts of Scotland. Draw or write about any wild animals that you have seen.

You won't find camels in Scotland except in safari parks and zoos. This family lives in Blair Drummond Safari Park, near Stirling.